# caillou®

## Goes Birdwatching

Adapted from
the animated series:
Francine Allen
Illustrations:
CINAR Animation

chouette    CINAR®

Grandma had
promised to take
Caillou birdwatching
today.

"Hurry up, Grandma!
Let's go!" Caillou
cried impatiently.
Grandma put on
her hat and coat.
"No need to rush,
Caillou. The birds
are always there."

Caillou and
Grandma walked
for quite a while.
"I don't see any
birds!" complained
Caillou.
"We should see
some, with all these
trees around. Look
carefully."

Suddenly, Caillou spotted
a whole flock of birds
swooping through the sky.
"Grandma! Over there!
I see them! Lots of them!"

Caillou and Grandma approached quietly.
They sat down on a bench near the tree
where the birds had landed.

Grandma brought out a package of birdseed and poured some into Caillou's hands.

"This is what they like best. Put some on the ground and watch. I bet we'll have some company before long."

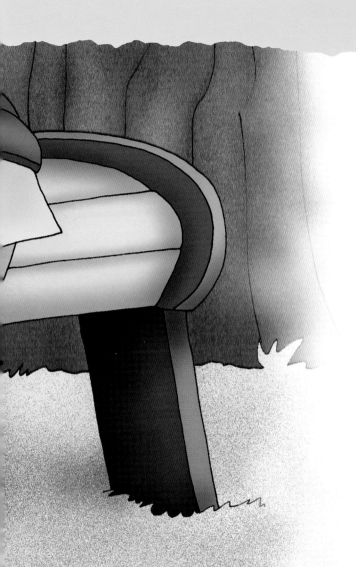

Caillou and Grandma sat
perfectly still. Very soon,
a little bird landed nearby.
"Look, Grandma!" exclaimed
Caillou. "The bird's eating
our seed!"

Excited, Caillou jumped up
and ran toward the bird.
He frightened the bird and
it flew away.

"Hey, little bird! Come back!"
cried Caillou.
"Let him go, Caillou. Birds are
afraid of big people like us.
We have to stand very still
and be very quiet so we don't
frighten them."

Caillou looked
at his grandmother
in amazement.
She knew so much!

Soon, another bird came and pecked at the seeds.
Then, more and more arrived. Caillou couldn't believe his eyes.
All kinds of birds!

"The red one is a cardinal," whispered Grandma.
"What about the little gray one with the black head?"
"Oh, that's a chickadee. They're very friendly birds."

Grandma poured more seed into Caillou's hands.
"Hold out your hands and stand very still," she told him.
Caillou didn't move. He watched the little chickadee hop
from branch to branch, getting closer and closer.

Suddenly, just as Caillou had
hoped, the bird left the tree
and landed in his hands!
Caillou looked at Grandma,
wide-eyed. He kept very
quiet because he didn't want
to scare the chickadee.
At last, the bird flew away
and Caillou cried out,
"Grandma! The chickadee
ate right out of my hand!"

On their way home, Caillou and Grandma listened to the birds singing. "Hear that? The little birds are talking to each other," said Grandma.

"Can I talk to them too?"

"Of course," replied Grandma. And she started to whistle.
Caillou tried too.
"Not bad, Caillou!" said Grandma with a smile. "You'll get it,
with a bit of practice."

Back home, Caillou
told his whole family
about the friendly little
chickadee. He loved
birdwatching.

Grandma had a surprise for Caillou. She gave him a little house, full of birdseed.

"It's a bird feeder," she explained.
"Do you think the birds will come to it?" Caillou asked.
"If we find a good place to hang it, I think they will," Grandma replied.

Grandma and Caillou decided to hang the feeder on the back porch.

"This is the perfect spot," said Grandma. "It's quiet, sunny, and, best of all, you can watch the birds from inside the house without disturbing them." "I hope my friend the chickadee comes for a visit!" Caillou laughed.

Text adapted by Francine Allen from the scenario taken from the CAILLOU animated film series produced by CINAR Corporation (© 1997 Caillou Productions Inc., a subsidiary of CINAR Corporation). All rights reserved.
Original scenario written by Marie-France Landry.
Illustrations taken from the television series CAILLOU.
Graphic design: Monique Dupras
Computer graphics: Les Studios de la Souris Mécanique


Canadian Cataloguing in Publication Data

Allen, Francine, 1955-
Caillou goes birdwatching
(Backpack Series)
Translation of: Caillou observe les oiseaux
For children aged 3 and up.
Co-published by Chouette Publishing (1987) Inc. and CINAR Corporation.

ISBN 2-89450-229-X

1. Fear - Juvenile literature. I. CINAR Corporation. II. Title. III. Series.

QL676.2.A4413 2001          j598'.07'234          C00-941725-7

Legal deposit: 2001

We gratefully acknowledge the financial support of BPIDP, SODEC, and the Canada Council for the Arts for our publishing activities.

Printed in Canada